TEENY WEENIES

THE BOY WHO CRIED WOOL

AND OTHER STORIES

STARSCAPE BOOKS BY DAVID LUBAR

Novels

Flip

Hidden Talents

True Talents

Monsterrific Tales

Hyde and Shriek

The Vanishing Vampire

The Unwilling Witch

The Wavering Werewolf

The Gloomy Ghost

The Bully Bug

Nathan Abercrombie, Accidental Zombie Series

My Rotten Life

Dead Guy Spy

Goop Soup

The Big Stink

Enter the Zombie

Story Collections

Attack of the Vampire Weenies and Other Warped and Creepy Tales

The Battle of the Red Hot Pepper Weenies and Other Warped and Creepy Tales

Beware the Ninja Weenies and Other Warped and Creepy Tales

Check out the Library Weenies and Other Warped and Creepy Tales

The Curse of the Campfire Weenies and Other Warped and Creepy Tales

In the Land of the Lawn Weenies and Other Warped and Creepy Tales

Invasion of the Road Weenies and Other Warped and Creepy Tales

Strikeout of the Bleacher Weenies and Other Warped and Creepy Tales

Wipeout of the Wireless Weenies and Other Warped and Creepy Tales

Teeny Weenies: Freestyle Frenzy and Other Stories

Teeny Weenies: The Intergalactic Petting Zoo and Other Stories

Teeny Weenies: My Favorite President and Other Stories

THE BOY WHO CRIED WOOL

AND OTHER STORIES

DAVID LUBAR

ILLUSTRATED BY BILL MAYER

STARSCAPE

A TOM DOHERTY ASSOCIATES BOOK
NEW YORK

THE BOY WHO CRIED WOOL AND OTHER STORIES

Copyright © 2019 by David Lubar

Illustrations copyright © 2019 by Bill Mayer

A Starscape Book
Published by Tom Doherty Associates
120 Broadway
New York, NY 10271

www.tor-forge.com

The Library of Congress Cataloging-in-Publication Data
is available upon request.

ISBN 978-1-250-17349-2 (hardcover)
ISBN 978-1-250-18776-5 (ebook)

Our books may be purchased in bulk for promotional, educational, or business use. Please contact your local bookseller or the Macmillan Corporate and Premium Sales Department at 1-800-221-7945, extension 5442, or by email at MacmillanSpecialMarkets@macmillan.com.

First Edition: September 2019

Printed in the United States of America

0 9 8 7 6 5 4 3 2 1

For Joelle and Alison,
the centers of my universe.

THE BOY WHO CRIED WOOL

AND OTHER STORIES

THE BOY WHO CRIED, "WOOL!"

The Aldritch family was on vacation. They'd driven their camper to a gorgeous campsite in an area called *Mammoth Hills*. The leaves were just turning their fall colors, and the air was crisp and cool enough to make long hikes comfortable. Mr. and Mrs. Aldritch loved camping. So did their two oldest children, Mark and Mandy. Their next oldest child, Teagan, didn't care about camping either way, but she definitely didn't like what happened every time the family went anywhere.

"Teagan," Mrs. Aldritch said as she laced up her hiking books. "I expect you to keep an eye on your little brother."

"But, Mom—" Teagan said.

"Listen to your mother," Mr. Aldritch said as he tucked his flannel shirt into his sturdy jeans. "Keep an eye on Conrad."

Teagan stared at her father, hoping for a bit of mercy. She got nothing. Once again, she was stuck watching the youngest member of the family.

As they headed away from their campsite toward the trail, Teagan whispered to Conrad, "Please behave. Okay? I don't want to have to chase you all over the woods."

Conrad, who was a bit overloaded with excess energy, didn't answer his sister. Instead, he flung his hand out, pointing ahead of the family, and screamed, "Woooooollll—"

"Shush," Teagan said, clamping a hand over her little brother's mouth. They'd gone to a petting zoo the other week, and Conrad had been scared by the sheep. Teagan waited until she was sure there would be no more shouting, then relaxed her grip and led Conrad along.

Ten minutes later, it happened again.

"Wooooollllll—" Conrad started to scream.

Teagan clamped down again and looked around. Far off, near the crest of a tall hill, she saw something that might have been a sheep. Or maybe it was a mountain goat. Whatever it was, there was no reason to be scared.

"Calm down, okay?" she said. "They won't hurt you."

Conrad nodded.

Teagan dropped her hand. "I don't get it," Teagan said. "You're so quiet at home."

Her little brother could sit all day looking at books about dinosaurs and prehistoric times. He'd stare at a drawing of a pterodactyl or a cave bear for hours. But get him outside, and he ran around and shouted like he was being chased by a pack of zombies.

Conrad screamed again at the base of the hill.

"Woooollll—"

Teagan looked up as she silenced her little brother. It had gotten a bit foggy. "Maybe we should turn back," Teagan said. Conrad's fear was making her nervous.

"Nonsense," her dad said. "The trail is well marked. The view at the top is supposed to be spectacular. We might even see a bald eagle."

"And we aren't quitters," her mom said.

They hiked up the hillside. Near the top, Teagan saw Conrad tense up his whole body. She reached out to silence him. But then, she decided she'd had enough.

"I'm just going to let him scream," she

said. Maybe then her parents would appreciate what she had to deal with.

It turned out Conrad had more to say than
just *wool*.

"Woooolllllymammmmmoth!!!!!" Conrad
screamed.

He'd finally managed to get the whole name
out. He'd spotted it way back, because he had
better vision than the rest of his family. And it
had terrified him. He'd been too scared to say
much, and his sister hadn't helped by stopping him every time he'd managed to speak.

There was no stopping him now. He
screamed the warning again.

And there was no stopping the
wooly mammoth. It charged down
the hill. So did the rest of its family,
which was also enjoying a lovely
walk among the colorful trees in
the crisp autumn air.

The Aldritches got knocked silly as the
herd stampeded past them. Except for Conrad,
who had the sense to leap out of the way and
not stand there staring with his mouth open.

Eventually, bruised, battered, and aching, the Aldritch family managed to get back to their tents, which had been trampled flat.

They never went camping again.

And from that day on, Teagan always listened to whatever Conrad had to say.

ALL YOU CAN EAT

Roddy Vangorf loved candy. So it was no surprise he loved Halloween. Roddy was also one of the laziest kids ever born. So it was also no surprise, despite his love of candy, that he hated having to walk door-to-door all over his neighborhood and beyond to get a sackful of sweets. Even worse, he had to put on a stupid mask.

Then, five years ago, Roddy got a late start going out for trick-or-treating. He'd only gone one block and had hardly gotten close to having enough candy for even a single night, when he stopped to lean against a tree and rest. Unfortunately for them, three other kids also decided to rest, right down the street. A ghost, a soldier, and a pirate stopped walking and put their bags down.

Roddy wasn't interested in the other kids. But he was interested in the bags. They bulged like the inflated cheeks of a trumpet player.

"That's a ton of candy," Roddy whispered. He couldn't peel his eyes away from the bags. "Maybe two tons."

He leaned away from the tree and crouched over. "They have more than they need."

Like a panther, Roddy sped down the street toward the three kids. Without even pausing, he snatched up one of the bags and flew past the victims.

He was half a block away, and darting between a pair of houses, before the three kids even seemed to notice they'd been

robbed of one-third of their candy.

Their cries of "Stop!" and "Hey!" barely reached Roddy's ears as he skittered across a backyard. Soon enough, he was tucked safely in his room, with his treasure spilled out on the floor in front of him.

He didn't feel an ounce of guilt as he tore the wrapper from a chocolate bar and crammed it into his eager mouth. He felt wonderful.

A year later, he decided to re-peat his perfect Halloween tech-nique. It didn't take Roddy long to spot a group of six superheroes. Spider-Man was lagging behind the rest of the group. He kept switching his bulg-ing sack of candy from hand to hand.

"I'll save you," Roddy said. He smiled at his cleverness. He was going to rescue Spidey from the agony of lugging all that sweet good-ness.

He took off, pushed himself to full speed, and snatched the bag right out of the weary hands of the solitary superhero.

He did it every year after that, though he was careful to pull off the snatch in a differ-ent part of town each time, so nobody would be expecting it. Halloween was definitely the best day of the year for Roddy. And when it rolled around again, he could hardly wait to stalk the streets and hunt for the best victim with the biggest bag of goodies.

And there they were. Two kids. A boy and a girl, dressed as wizards. Each toted an overloaded bag of treats. Roddy slipped behind them, keeping enough distance so they wouldn't spot him if they looked back.

"Which one?" he asked himself.

The answer was obvious and so glorious that it made him cackle. There was no reason to choose. He'd grab both bags. That would give him more candy than he'd ever gotten before. A trickle of drool rolled down his chin as he thought about taking that first delicious bite.

It didn't bother him at all that this would leave the little wizards with nothing. That was their problem.

Roddy put on a burst of speed and shot between the kids, snatching both bags with the speed and accuracy of a striking snake.

 He was nearly a block away when he realized something was missing. There hadn't been a shout. That was strange. The cry of dismay was almost as sweet as the candy. What was wrong with these kids?

Roddy spun around. And then, he froze in place. The kids both stood there, each calmly pointing at him with one hand. They each placed their other hand on their stomachs. But that wasn't the creepiest part. They were right in front of him! It was like they'd kept up with him as he'd run away. But that was impossible. He'd heard no other footsteps striking the sidewalk. And he'd darted past them at full speed.

Finally, they spoke.

"Eat it all."

Just three words. But those three words seemed to leave their mouths like ropes and wrap around Roddy's chest so tightly he had to struggle to breathe.

He was so spooked, he dropped the bags.

Or, at least, he tried to. His fingers wouldn't move. His hands wouldn't open.

He turned and fled.

On the way home, he tried flinging the candy from the bags. The pieces were wedged inside. He couldn't get rid of them.

When he reached his room, his fingers went slack. The bags dropped, spilling their contents across the floor.

Eat it all.

The words came from the walls and window. They came from the floor. They came from Roddy's bed and from his clothes.

He ran to his door.

It wouldn't open.

He banged at it and screamed for help.

Nobody heard. Nobody came.

Eat it all.

Roddy ate candy.

He tried to enjoy it. But terror does not blend well with licorice. Fear does not improve the flavor of caramels. Horror drains the sweetness from gummy bears.

He ate.

Time passed.

He begged to be set free.

Eat it all was the only response.

Finally, after a forever of gorging, after an unbearable period of cramming his mouth with the gruesome sweets, struggling to swallow and fighting not to throw up, he ate the last piece.

"It's done," Roddy said in a voice somewhere between a gasp and a moan. He stood, shakily, and walked toward his door. His stomach dragged at him like it held fifty pounds of thick stew.

The door opened before he could get there.

"You're not done," the wizards said. They stood in the hall. Each held one handle of a bag. Roddy recognized the bag. He'd stolen it one year ago.

The wizards placed the bag on the floor and stepped back into the hall.

"No. Please . . . ," Roddy said.

Eat it all.

Roddy reached into the bag and tried not to think about how many more there were to come.

BUSTING PUMPKINS

Albert Gorfesh loved to smash things. It didn't matter whether it was his own thing that got smashed or somebody else's. If he could hurl it to the ground and watch it shatter into pieces, he was happy. His friends didn't share that feeling. Actually, his friends drifted off or fled, one by one, until only Stan Wample was left. Stan was a follower. He had no thoughts of his own. So he was happy to do whatever Albert did.

Albert also hated holidays.

Two weeks before Halloween, as they were walking through their neighborhood, Albert grabbed Stan's arm in one hand, pointed across the street with the other, and said, "Pumpkins!"

Stan followed the path of the pointing finger and saw a single pumpkin on a porch. There was a lopsided grin carved into its face. "So?"

"I'll bet they're great to smash," Albert said. His own lopsided smile mirrored that of the pumpkin.

"I'll bet they are, too," Stan said.

Albert's smile grew bigger as he pictured the sight and sound of the pumpkin being hurled to the hard concrete of the sidewalk.

"Are we going to smash it now?" Stan asked. He took a step toward the porch.

"Oh yeah," Albert said. Then, a thought stopped him in his tracks. "No! Wait. That's the Fullers' house. They always decorate early. They had their Christmas lights up last year in November. And they had stuff for St. Patrick's Day by the middle of February."

"But why wait?" Stan asked.

"Because there are a lot more pumpkins coming. If I smash this one, everybody will be watching for it to happen again." Albert was an expert on how to not get caught— mostly because he'd been caught so many times. "If we wait until the night before Halloween, we can smash every pumpkin in the neighborhood. It will be amazing!"

"Yeah . . ." Stan's mouth hung open as he tried to absorb the idea of smashing endless pumpkins. "Let's wait."

And so they waited. As Halloween grew closer, more and more pumpkins appeared on porches and front walkways. There were tiny ones and giant ones. There were amazing works of art and crude carvings.

Albert trembled with anticipation as he imagined smashing each and every one. He'd

chuck the small ones like baseballs. He'd lift the huge ones with Stan's help. They'd smash everything in one glorious path of destruction.

He could hardly wait.

The night before Halloween, Albert met Stan at the far end of their block.

"Shhh," Albert said, lifting a finger to his lips.

Stan nodded. And then, unnecessarily, he lifted a finger to his own lips and returned the shush.

They crept up the first porch.

"Your time has come," Albert whispered.

He and Stan each grabbed one of the two pumpkins sitting there. They crept to the street, exchanged glances, nodded, and flung their pumpkins to the road.

The pumpkins smashed gloriously. Albert almost let out a whoop of joy. He'd been waiting so long for this moment, he couldn't believe it was finally here. The two of them raced to the next porch. And the next. They worked their way down the street, smashing every pumpkin. They left a trail of broken pieces behind them.

They moved down the street.

So did the broken pieces.

Tendrils of fiber reached out like tentacles, dragging the shattered pieces down the street. Tiny fragments, large hunks, and everything between slid along the road, following the boys and pulling together. As Albert and Stan reached the last house and smashed the last pumpkin, they found themselves facing two towering patchwork pumpkins.
Each had a pair of gaping holes the size of manhole covers for eyes. Each had a grin that grew wider now that their time had come.

Albert craned his neck back, trying to see the top of them. So did Stan. The gigantic pumpkins rotated so their eyes faced each other. The pumpkins tilted forward as if nodding in agreement. Then they rotated back to face their victims, and they leaped straight up in the air.

They came down on Albert and Stan, smashing the pumpkin smashers. A lot of damage was done. Albert had seventeen broken bones. Stan had twelve. Neither was in any shape to smash anything for quite a while. And when the next Halloween rolled around, they both decided it was best not to go outside at all.

THE SOCK
DRAWER

We dumped our bags on the floor of my bedroom and stared at all the candy.

"Best Halloween ever," my friend Peter said.

"For sure," his sister, Cindy, said. She pointed at my pile. "Hey, Andrea, what's that?"

I looked down. There, among the candy bars and boxes, I saw a pen. It was attached to a piece of cardboard with the words *Halloween Magic Pen* on it.

"No idea." I peeled back the cardboard and pulled out the pen. "Did you get one?"

"Nope," Cindy said.

"Me either." Peter held his hand out. "Let me try it."

I gave him the pen. He was the best artist in our group. Before I could hand him a piece of paper, he leaned over and drew something on his sock. We were all wearing white socks as part of our soccer-player costumes. I watched his drawing take shape. It was a spider.

"Perfect for Halloween," he said.

"Your mom's not going to like that," I said.

"She won't care. She's always telling me to express myself." He passed the pen to Cindy. "Here. Draw something."

"Like what?" she asked.

"Something Halloweenish," Peter said.

"You mean *Halloweenie*," I said.

Cindy giggled. "No. That's us. We're Halloweenies. A bat is Halloweenish. Yeah! That's what I'll draw." She leaned over and drew a bat on her sock. It wasn't as good as Peter's spider, but it was good enough that anyone could tell what she'd made.

She slid the pen to me. "Your turn."

I picked up the pen and stared at my sock. I liked monsters. I decided to draw a vampire. It came out looking pretty good, so I drew a second one on my other sock. "Check it out," I said when I was finished.

"Not bad," Peter said.

"But I don't see any magic," Cindy said. "It's supposed to be magic. Maybe there are instructions." She picked up the cardboard from the pen and turned it over. There, in big, red letters, I saw: WARNING. DO NOT DRAW ON CLOTHING!

"Oops," Peter said. "Too late."

"No big deal," I said. I had plenty of socks.

Peter got this funny look on his face. Then he screamed and started yanking at his socks. They seemed to fall apart in his hands. Then I screamed when I realized they weren't falling apart. They were turning into spiders. Dozens of them.

Cindy screamed, too. But not just because of the spiders. A tiny bat was frantically flapping its wings between her foot and her sneaker. She yanked the sneaker off. The bat flew out of the room.

I stared at my socks. There was no way they'd turn into vampires. I was relieved to see they weren't changing shape. And even if they did, they'd be small.

My relief vanished when I felt sharp stings in both feet, like someone was biting me. Red dots appeared by the fangs. I tried to look away, but the vampire's eyes locked onto me. I watched as the dots grew as large as pennies and then quarters. Finally, the red blotches reached the hypnotic eyes and covered them.

"Get them off!" I yelled as I tore my gaze away from the vampire's. The room started to spin. I was feeling faint. I tried to reach for my socks, but I couldn't seem to make my hands do what I wanted. I flopped down on my back.

"Help . . . ," I said. My voice was just a whisper now.

Peter and Cindy dived on my feet and ripped off the socks. I barely managed to keep from passing out.

Peter grabbed an empty can that had held potato chips and shoved the socks in there, then slapped the lid back on. They helped me to my feet. I looked down and saw fang marks.

"Do you think I'll turn into a vampire?" I asked.

"You're more likely to turn into a sock," Peter said.

I was going to tell him that wasn't funny. But I realized it was. By then, all of the spiders had scurried away. We went downstairs and opened the door so the bat could fly out. Then Peter opened the can and tossed the socks in the fireplace, where my parents had a roaring fire going.

I was pretty nervous that night when I

went to sleep. I was afraid I'd wake up as a vampire. But I didn't. So I guess it all could have been a lot worse. Whenever I look back, I think about all the other things I could have drawn—snakes, alligators, *Tyrannosaurus rex*—and I shudder a bit.

I also make sure I always read the back of any package before I open it.

LEAVE IT BE

dwin stepped out on his front porch and felt the cool breeze that marked the change of seasons. It was the first day of autumn, Edwin's favorite season. The leaves on the maple tree next to the porch were already starting to turn colors. Soon, Edwin knew he'd be kicking through piles of leaves. Soon after that, he'd get to go out for Halloween, and after that, he'd stuff himself with turkey, gravy, and mashed potatoes. Sure, summer was great for swimming and baseball, but he'd had enough bright sunshine and double plays for now. He was ready for corn mazes and caramel apples.

"Fall!" Edwin shouted, loving even the sound of that word.

A rustling like a thousand startled birds filled the air. Leaves fell. Every leaf on the sugar maple next to the porch turned to shades of red, yellow, or orange and then let loose from the branches. The leaves fluttered to the ground.

Edwin stared at the bare limbs of the maple tree and at the colorful carpet on the lawn. *Did I do that?* he wondered. He stepped down from the porch and walked to the next nearest tree, a large oak on the corner of the front yard.

"Fall!" Edwin shouted.

The oak leaves turned color and fell. Edwin dashed under the tree and spun around in the shower of leaves, flinging his arms wide and laughing.

When the rain of leaves ended, Edwin ran into the

neighbor's yard, where three birch trees surrounded a large rock. Edwin climbed up on the rock, at the center of a triangle formed by the trees.

"Fall!" he shouted.

Leaves fell from all three trees, showering Edwin in another magical moment.

 He hopped off the rock and dashed for the next house.

"What are you doing?"

The shout came from behind him. Edwin looked over his shoulder. His sister, Irene, was chasing after him.

"I'm making fall," he said. "Watch." He slid to a stop by a tree at the curb. "Fall!"

Leaves fell.

"Maybe you shouldn't do that," Irene said.

"It's fun," Edwin said. He ran to the next tree.

"It's not natural," Irene said.

"You're just mad because I can do it," Edwin said. He made his way around the block, dropping the leaves from every single tree. Finally, he reached the very last untouched tree on the block. He stood  right under it, staring up at all the leaves that would soon cascade down on him like confetti at a parade.

"Don't do it," Irene said.

Edwin did it.

"Fall!" he shouted.

The leaves fell. In a moment, the tree stood bare like every other tree on the block.

The sun seemed to grow dimmer. Clouds filled the sky. The air changed from cool to chilly, and then from chilly to bitter cold.

Edwin shivered.

Instead of leaves, something else  fell.

Snow.

Flurries of cold, white flakes filled the air. Fall was over. It had come and gone in less than a day, thanks to Edwin.

It was winter now.

Irene loved winter. She loved it even more

than Edwin loved fall. She wanted to shout, "Snow!" But she knew enough not to say anything. She wanted to enjoy winter one day at a time.

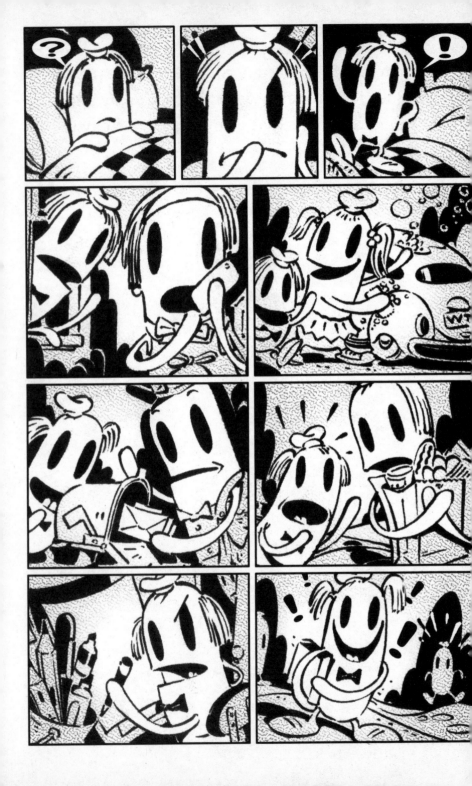

ESTHER'S SENTENCE

It was a sunny Saturday morning. But it felt just like every other sunny Saturday morning. Esther woke up in the same bed in the same room in the same house under the same sun as always.

I need to do something different today, Esther thought as she got ready to go eat the same Saturday breakfast she always ate.

She thought about putting her clothes on backward. That would be different, but mostly it would just be silly. She thought about walking to the Amazon River and fishing for giant catfish. That would be different, but she wasn't

 allowed to cross the street by
herself. She thought about
learning to speak French.
That would be different, but
she was pretty sure it would
take more than one morning
to learn the whole language.
Esther realized that whatever she did, she'd
better do it in a language she already knew.

"I've got it!" Esther said as the idea hit her.
"I'll say something that has never ever been
said before."

Esther stood on her bed, puffed
out her chest, and said, "The
ant dragged the piano to the
carpenter." It sure sounded
like something no one had ever
said. Just to be sure, Esther
added a few more words: "The
purple ant dragged the soft piano
to the grumpy carpenter."

Esther figured that the sentence would
want to be heard. If she were words, she knew
she'd want to be heard. She ran downstairs to

the kitchen and told her mother, "The purple ant dragged the soft piano to the grumpy carpenter."

But her mother was on the telephone, and the sentence just went in one ear and out the other. That wasn't an easy trip.

"I'm sorry," Esther said to the sentence after it had wriggled its way free. "But don't worry—I'll take care of you. You have my word."

Esther rushed to the living room, where her brother was watching television. She caught her breath, then said, "The purple ant dragged the soft piano to the grumpy carpenter."

But her brother was so fascinated with his program that talking to him was like talking to a brick wall. The collision hurt the little string of words. First, it went in one ear and out the other; now, it had bounced off a brick wall.

"Maybe we should go outside," Esther said to the sentence as it landed with a clatter at her feet. She walked out the door. The sentence, which couldn't say anything other than what it was already saying, mumbled along next to her.

Esther ran up to her big sister, who was washing the car in the driveway, and told her, "The purple ant dragged the soft piano to the grumpy carpenter."

But her sister was using the hose to spray the hubcaps, and the water made such a roar that Esther's sentence was lost in all the noise.

"Oh no," Esther said as she hunted for her sentence. Finally, she spotted it in a puddle of soapy water. She picked it up and dried it off on her shirt, then put it back on the ground.

As Esther walked toward the front lawn, she heard familiar footsteps. She saw the mailman coming up the street. Surely someone who delivered letters would appreciate the sentence.

Esther dashed over to him and said, "The purple ant dragged the soft piano to the grumpy carpenter." The mailman heard the words, but he had other thoughts in his head, and he pushed the sentence from his mind.

Ouch! The poor sentence had gone in one ear and out the other, bounced off a brick wall, gotten lost, and then been pushed. It plopped to the ground and whimpered along behind Esther, trying not to fall apart.

Esther was almost sorry that she had ever said the sentence. But it was in such a poor condition that she didn't dare let it know how she felt. The words seemed to be losing their shape and meaning. The word *purple* was fading to a pale gray, and *soft* was turning into mush.

Poor sentence, Esther thought, wondering if she would have to send it out on its own. Then she saw Mrs. Severance, her next-door neighbor, standing on her porch. Esther rushed up to her and started to say, "The purple ant dragged the soft—"

"I can't listen to you right now, Esther; I have important things to do," she said, breaking Esther off in the middle of the sentence. This was the worst of all. After going in one ear and out the other, bouncing off a brick wall, getting lost, and being pushed, the poor sentence had been broken.

Esther gathered the pieces and carried them to her room. She put the shattered sentence on her bed. She hoped it would pull itself together, but it just lay there without making any attempt to express itself. Bruised and broken and hurt and shivering, the sentence was ready to disappear.

"Don't give up," Esther said. "I have an idea."

 Her grandmother had given her a fountain pen. This was the old-fashioned type of pen that used ink from a bottle. Esther took the pen from the desk and carefully sucked up the sentence. Then she wrote it down, without that painful break, on a page in her notebook. The words flowed smoothly

onto the paper. In a minute, the ink was dry and the sentence was safe.

"There," Esther told it, "no one is ever going to bounce or bruise or lose or break or push you again."

She closed the notebook, keeping the sentence snug and secure. She didn't tell it, but she had a surprise planned for Sunday morning. When the sentence was all rested from its adventures and feeling well again, Esther was going to write another sentence to keep it company. And that new sentence just might be one that had never ever been written before.

THE HORN
OF PLENTY

Linda saw the horn in a garbage can at the curb, five blocks from her house. It was lying there, glittering, half-hidden among orange peels, coffee grounds, and other things best left unidentified.

"You're throwing that out?" she asked the woman who had just rolled the can to the curb.

"I don't need it anymore," the woman said. "My children are grown. I don't know anyone else who would want it."

"What is it?" Linda asked.

"A cornucopia," the woman said, "or a horn

of plenty. It produces endless good things. We used to put it on the table every Thanksgiving, when my children were young and living at home."

"Endless good things? I'd want that! Can I have it?" Linda asked. Even half-buried by trash, the horn was lovely. It looked like a ram's horn, with a big opening at the end. And if it produced good things, all the better.

"You shouldn't pick through garbage," the woman said. She stood there, with no expression on her face, waiting for Linda to move on.

Linda did move on. But she crept back as soon as it got dark and snatched the horn from the garbage can. She'd even thought to wear a pair of the rubber gloves her parents used when they had to clean the drain in the bathroom sink or touch other icky things.

The next morning, she cleaned the horn. It gleamed. Linda hadn't totally believed the horn would produce good things. Not back when the woman had first told her. But now, looking at it, and seeing  the way it shimmered, she was sure it was magic. Better yet, tomorrow was Thanksgiving. She'd put the horn on the table and see what happened.

Her parents stared at her for a moment the next afternoon when she brought the horn from her room. But they let her put it on the table.

Nothing came out at first. But when Linda was about to enjoy her second helping of turkey and gravy, a strange sound caught her attention. The horn buzzed, like it was warming up and getting ready to stream out a series of surprises.

"Watch this," she told her parents.

The buzzing grew louder.

She pointed at the horn. "You'll be amazed."

Her parents leaned forward.

The horn buzzed so hard, it started to vibrate.

"Any second now . . . ," Linda said.

A fly came out.

And then another.

And then a hundred more.

"Get that thing out of here!" her dad screamed.

Linda grabbed the horn and ran from the house. She tried to throw the horn away. The thin end wrapped around her wrist like a handcuff. She couldn't break free. More flies streamed out. They swarmed around her. Linda raced down the street. Something told her that she had to bring it back to where she'd gotten it.

She reached the house. The can was gone. She went to the porch and banged on the door.

When the woman answered, Linda shoved the horn at her. "Here! Take it! You told me good things would come out. You lied!"

The horn released its grip on her.

"They are good," the woman said as the swarm of flies grew even thicker. "My children love them. And my children came for a surprise visit. So I guess I can use this again." She plucked the horn from Linda, then turned away and called, "Come here, my children."

Past her, Linda saw dozens of dark shapes emerging from another room. They scurried and scuttled on eight legs. The woman thrust more arms through slits in her dress. She had eight arms, too. Or legs. Her eyes grew larger. Hairs sprouted on her limbs. She opened her mouth and inhaled flies. Her children, large spiders, joined her on the porch. They feasted on the flies.

Linda ran.

The spiders ran faster.

In the end, Linda had nothing to be thankful for.

TRICK AND TREAT

Halloween was always one of the best days of the year—unless it was also moving day. Micah, who loved Halloween, arrived in his new town at 4:30 in the afternoon. He was afraid the best night of the year was going to be ruined. He didn't even have a clue what route to take.

"I don't know anybody," he told his mom as she unpacked a box of books. "I'll have to go out by myself."

"I'm sure you'll make friends," she said.

"Not in time for Halloween," Micah said. He opened the front door and looked up and down the street. "I don't even see any kids. Wait! There's something else I don't see, either."

Micah ran outside, hoping he was wrong. He dashed to one end of the block and then to the other. "Nothing!" he said. There wasn't a single pumpkin, skeleton, or vampire in sight. No decorations on doors. No tombstones on lawns. No skeletons dangling from trees.

"I don't think they celebrate Halloween here," he told his dad, who was putting dishes away in a cabinet.

"Of course they do," his dad said.

As the skies grew dark and the air filled with an autumn chill, Micah realized he had another problem. He didn't have his costume.

"Where's my monster mask?" he asked his parents.

"It's somewhere," his dad said, pointing to the zillions of boxes stacked against the living room wall.

"You'll find it," his mom said.

Micah tried. The night got darker. He got desperate. He had a pair of plastic vampire teeth his best friend had given him for his birthday. He slipped them in his mouth, grabbed a black towel from the bathroom to use as a cape, found a plastic bag for the candy he hoped he'd collect, and said, "I'm going out."

"Have fun," his parents said.

Micah went to the sidewalk and looked around. There was nobody in sight. "This isn't Halloween," he said. Halloween was when the whole neighborhood was filled with kids in costumes. It was like having a hundred small parades going on in all directions at once.

He went to the house next door and knocked.

A man answered. "Yes?"

Micah looked past him. He didn't see a bowl of candy. "Trick or treat," he said.

"Sure," the man said. "Wait right here." He

dashed off, leaving Micah feeling just slightly more hopeful.

The man came back holding a deck of cards. He fanned them out and thrust them toward Micah. "Here. Pick a card. Any card."

"What?" Micah asked.

"You wanted a trick, right?" the man said.

"No!" Micah said. "I want a treat. Or *you'll* get tricked."

"Oh, I get it," the man said. He straightened up the deck and offered it to Micah. "Here. I love tricks. Show me one."

Micah let out a cry of frustration and walked away. "Trick or treat," he said at the next house.

"I'll take a treat," the woman said. "What do you have?"

Puzzled, frustrated, and sad, Micah slinked away from that house, too. And the next one. And the one after that. Nobody seemed to have a clue what day it was. Nobody seemed to understand the simple idea that they were supposed to give him candy. When he reached the end of the block and faced the last house, he told himself he was just about ready to quit. This would be the last one. If nobody there understood Halloween, he'd just have to give up.

Micah knocked on the door.

It swung open, revealing total darkness.

"Come in." The voice was deep and slow.

Micah hesitated. He knew better than to walk into a strange house— especially a strange house that was totally dark.

Orange-colored light flickered on the other side of the room. Candlelight filtered through two triangles and a gaping slit. It was a jack-o'-lantern. This was the first sign he'd seen this evening that Halloween existed in this town. Micah took a step toward it.

More lights switched on. The room was suddenly filled with light. And filled with people.

"Happy Halloween!" they all shouted.

They were all wearing costumes. Both the

kids and adults were dressed for Halloween. He spotted his parents off to one side, in prince and princess costumes.

"Welcome to the neighborhood," a man wearing a space helmet said.

His parents came over. His mom held out his costume. "When I told our new neighbors how much you loved Halloween, they decided your first Halloween in your new town should be one you'd never forget."

And that's exactly what it was. Micah knew he'd remember this night forever. He'd been tricked. But the trick was a real treat.

HAMMER IT OUT

All I saw at first was the tiniest tip of the handle. At that point, I didn't even know it was a handle. All I knew was something shiny caught my eye right off the trail in Bryland Woods. "Hey, what's that?" I asked, pointing with my fishing rod to a spot between two trees.

"What's what?" Ryley asked. He squinted toward where I was pointing.

"That," I said, jabbing my rod closer to it.

Ryley shrugged. I went over, dropped to my knees, and reached down to touch the shiny piece of metal.

"Whoa!" I jerked my hand back.

"What's wrong?" Ryley asked.

"Nothing." I took a breath and reached out again. I'd expected it to be cold. But it was warm. Not hot. Definitely not burning hot. But warmer than a piece of metal should be on the floor of the woods, in the shade of the trees, in the early morning.

I touched it again. Then I felt around it. I got my knife out of my tackle box and started to dig. That's when I realized the object was a handle. Soon after, I discovered it was attached to the head of a hammer.

"Wow," I said as I pulled it free from the ground. "Look at that."

"Man, that's not for hammering nails," Ryley said.

"You're right about that," I said. "I think it's some kind of war hammer."

"Great! You found it!"

Ryley and I spun toward the voice. A guy was standing there, right behind us. He was wearing sweatpants and a sweatshirt. He was skinny, with really long reddish-blond hair. He held his hand out.

I stepped back away from him and shook my head. "It's mine," I said.

He laughed and reached farther, stretching toward me.

"Hey!" I shouted as the hammer jerked against my grip. I clenched my fist and pulled my arm back. "Stop it!"

"That's not yours. It's mine," he said.

"Finders keepers," I said. I put my other hand on the head of the hammer and pulled it to my chest.

He thrust his hand even farther out. "Give it back!"

My fingers were slipping. Maybe it really was his. But this was no way to get it back. I didn't like the way he was trying to force it out of my hands. I knew I couldn't hold on much longer. Well, if he wanted it, I was going to let him have it.

I opened my fingers and shoved my hands out, flinging the hammer toward him. At the exact same time, he gritted his teeth and shouted even louder, "Come to me!"

The hammer flew from my hands and bonked him on the head.

He blinked hard, once.

"Are you okay?" I asked.

He blinked hard again.

"Mister, are you all right?" Ryley asked.

He didn't blink a third time. Instead, he flopped back and hit the ground.

"You killed him," Ryley said.

"No, I didn't!" I shouted it even though I wasn't sure he was wrong. But I could see that the guy was breathing. "He's not dead. Just knocked out."

The hammer was lying next

to him. I left it alone for the moment, knelt down, grabbed the guy's shoulder, and shook him. "Hey, wake up."

"Maybe we should just leave," Ryley said.

"We can't leave him here, knocked out in the woods," I said. "A bear might come along or something."

I shook him again.

He opened one eye. Then he sat up.

"Who are you?" I asked.

"I'm Thor," he said.

"Try using a heating pad," Ryley said.

The guy and I both stared at him. "Old joke," Ryley said.

"Not funny," the guy said. "I've heard that a million times."

"Thor," I said. "Like the Norse god of thunder?"

"Yeah, that's me."

"You don't look very much like a god," I said.

"I'm in human form," he said. "We do that

sometimes to pass among the mortals and perform heroic deeds."

"Like losing your hammer?" I asked.

"That was an accident," he said. "I got lost in the woods. Then I got tired and took a nap. Next thing I know, I wake up without my hammer."

I picked it up now. "Maybe you don't deserve it," I said.

He opened his mouth to argue, but then he sighed. "You could be right. I seem to lose it all the time. Things always go wrong when I come down here." He stopped and rubbed his forehead. I guess he was still a little dizzy from getting clunked by the hammer.

"Want me to hang on to it for you for a while?" I asked.

His eyes widened, and he studied me for a moment before speaking. "Would you?"

"Sure," I said.

"Thanks." He turned away from me and wandered off. And that's when the mortal-form spell I'd cast on my body and mind also wore off. I'd discovered over the millennia that it was so much more rewarding to experience things for the first time, even if I was actually experiencing them for the hundredth or ten thousandth time.

I waited until Thor was out of sight and savored the memory of the look on his face after he'd gotten clobbered. "That was fun," I said to Ryley.

"It's almost too easy," he said. "How many times have you done stuff like this to him?"

"Thousands," I said. "I've lost count."

"Don't you ever get tired of it?" he asked.

"Nope. I'm Loki, after all," I said. "I wouldn't be much of a god of mischief if I didn't play tricks on unsuspecting victims."

"You're much Lokier than he was," Ryley said.

"That's not funny," I said. "And I've

heard it a million times." But then I laughed. Because it was sort of funny. And if you can't laugh at yourself, you really can't do a good job laughing at others.

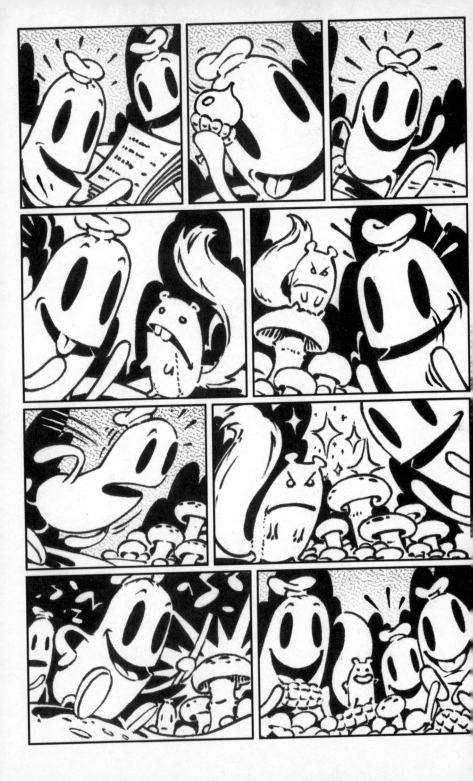

THE SILVER 'SHROOM

"Now, Quincy, I want you to behave today," Wenefer told her son. She was busily weaving dandelion stems into place mats for the banquet. Tonight, the elves were having the fall feast, the most important celebration of the year, and the tastiest.

"I'll try," Quincy said, spinning an acorn on the tip of his finger.

"And don't play with the food," Wenefer said, taking the acorn from him.

Quincy was bored. He wanted help with the feast. "Can I do anything?" he asked.

Wenefer stopped weaving and smiled at him. "If you wish, you may gather the mushrooms."

"Super!" Quincy said, running toward the woods.

"Be careful with them," his mother called after him.

Quincy did a few cartwheels and a somersault on his way to the mushroom patch. It was wonderful having such an important job. Mushrooms were the best part of the feast. And these mushrooms would be extremely good. The most skilled gardener among all the elves, Putterswoop, had tended the patch himself. These mushrooms would be delicious.

Too bad Putterswoop can't be here, Quincy thought. He had gone to the other side of Tall Cedar Woods to try to stop the trolls from making war with the gnomes. The elves did their best to keep peace in the woods.

"What's the hurry?" The voice came from behind Quincy.

"Hello, Zipper," Quincy said, turning to

see the small gray squirrel who was his friend.

 "I'm going to gather mushrooms for the feast."

"Ick," Zipper said. "I don't see how you can eat those things. Acorns, yes—mushrooms, no."

The squirrel caught up to Quincy with three quick hops, then loped along beside him. "I didn't know it was time for the feast."

"I guess that's because Putterswoop isn't here," the elf said. "He usually spreads the word."

"That explains it." Zipper ran ahead of Quincy, then skittered to a stop by the mushroom patch. Looking over his shoulder, he asked, "Have you learned any new tricks recently?"

"I sure did," Quincy told him. "I learned to turn leaves into silver. Watch this." Walking toward Zipper, Quincy pointed at a leaf at the edge of a branch on a hickory tree.

He started to speak the magic words he had learned. The tip of his finger tingled  as the power built up. Right before he reached the last word, he tripped on a twig.

"Oof," he said, hitting the ground.

"Are you all right?" Zipper asked.

"I'm fine," Quincy said. "I didn't get—" The rest of the sentence froze in his throat when he saw what he had done. One of the mushrooms, one of Putterswoop's special and cherished mushrooms, had turned to silver. "Oh no! Now I've done it."

"Why don't you just turn it back?" Zipper asked.

"I don't know how," Quincy moaned. There were only five mushrooms in the patch—just enough to go around when sliced very thin. Now, one of them was silver and definitely not fit to eat. He knew his mother would be angry.

"This always happens to me," Quincy said. "I don't mean to do anything wrong, but somehow I mess everything up."

"You may as well make the best of it," Zipper said. "There are still four left."

Quincy gathered the mushrooms. Then he told the squirrel, "I don't think you should come back with me. I wouldn't want you to get into trouble, too." Putting the four regular mushrooms together, and hiding the silver one in the middle, Quincy tied the bundle with pieces of grass. Then he headed back. He didn't want to go, but he knew there was no use stalling.

His mother didn't look up when he approached. As he got closer, he saw that she was staring down at an unfinished place mat. He'd never seen her look so sad.

"What's wrong?" he asked.

"You might as well forget about them," his mother said, pointing at the mushrooms. "There isn't going to be a feast."

Quincy dropped his bundle. This was terrible news. "Why not?"

"Diggleby came by right after you left. He had no idea it was time for the feast," Wenefer said. "That didn't worry me at first, because he'd just returned from the Shadow Realm. But Rinzer and Mayblue, who were just here, had no idea, either. And they hadn't gone anywhere."

"How could they not know?" Quincy asked.

"When Putterswoop left, he was in such a rush that he forgot to ask anyone to call the elves together," Wenefer said. "You know they never remember to come unless they're reminded. Nobody knows that the feast is tonight, and it's too late to find everyone now."

"That's terrible," Quincy said. It would be feast time in several hours. The elves in his home, Sunnyknoll Patch, had been preparing food all day. But with elves spread throughout the forest, there was no quick way to spread the word. Quincy looked at the mushrooms. His feeling of relief was quickly replaced with a wave of sadness. He wouldn't get into trouble now, but that didn't

seem to matter anymore. The silver mushroom was no longer important.

No, Quincy realized, the silver mushroom was suddenly very important!

"I'll get everyone here," he told his mother, untying the bundle. He took out the silver mushroom and set it on the ground.

"What in the world did you do this time?" his mother asked, staring at the shiny mushroom.

"You'll see." Quincy grabbed a stick and hit the mushroom. It rang clear as a bell. The 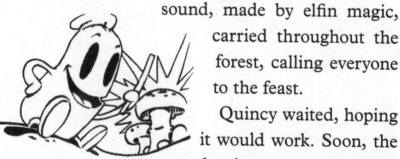 sound, made by elfin magic, carried throughout the forest, calling everyone to the feast.

Quincy waited, hoping it would work. Soon, the elves began to arrive. They came from near and far. Nobody minded getting a smaller portion of mushrooms than usual. It was better than having no portion at all. Besides, there were plenty of other things to eat.

As Quincy was starting his meal, Zipper came up to him.

"Say," the squirrel asked, "did I hear a dinner bell?"

"No," Quincy told him, inviting the squirrel to join the feast. "Actually, it was a dinner mushroom."

GOBBLE GOBBLE

As long as I can remember, my whole family had the most magical and special way to celebrate Thanksgiving. We don't eat turkey smothered in gravy or tangy spoonsful of cranberry sauce. We don't cram a slice of spicy pumpkin pie into our overstuffed stomachs or glug a thick and creamy glass of eggnog. We don't eat anything. At least, not before everyone else has had a chance to eat. Instead, we help serve food to less fortunate people. We all do: Mom, Dad, my older sister, Rebecca, and my little brothers, Cam and Oliver. And me, of course. I'm Rosalie.

We did this at the New Faith Food Shelter. People had been serving food to the hungry all day. By sunset, a lot of the volunteers were exhausted. That's when we liked to come. We'd show up at the back door, by the kitchen, and Pastor Michael would hand Dad the carving knife and Mom a big ladle.

"Thank you for coming," he'd say.

"We wouldn't miss it," Mom would say.

And we'd start serving food. I loved it. Whether I was scooping mashed potatoes or grabbing a serving of green beans with a pair of tongs, I liked working the hot line. That's what it's called—I guess because the food is hot.

And the people on the other side are great. Some of them don't have anywhere else to go. It feels good to help them. They're all humans, no matter how rich or poor.

But we also have to deal with human nature. Any time anything is free, you can count on someone being a cheater. They're easy to spot, even though they pretend to be needy. I don't know why they do it. But there are always people who come for a free meal when they could easily buy one for themselves.

That's just wrong. This year, I spotted one of them as soon as he stepped through the door. He was wearing a tattered jacket. But his shoes were new, and so was the watch that peeked past his frayed cuff. He looked at the food like someone who was about to snatch a purse.

I glanced at Mom and Dad. They nodded. We all exchanged glances, having a conversation with our eyes. Dad put a large slice of turkey on a plate for the man. Instead of handing the plate over right away, Dad asked, "More?"

"Yes. I'm very hungry," the man said.

I noticed he didn't say please. And when he got his plate, he didn't thank anyone. I kept an eye on him. As I'd expected, he rushed back to the line for seconds. Most people, no matter how hungry they are when they come in, won't ask for another helping until they know there's enough for everyone.

He stayed and ate until it was time to close up the shelter. I brought him some extra cranberry sauce. That's my favorite Thanks-giving food. It's like a dessert you can eat through the whole meal. Cam made sure the man got an extra-large slice of pumpkin pie. That's Cam's favorite. Our generosity might seem strange to anyone who doesn't know us, but we believe the more you give, the more you get back.

Finally, he left, waddling like a duck stuffed with marbles. So did we. We followed him down the street until he reached his car. It was very new and very expensive. He took off the jacket and tossed it in a trash can.

Then he got in his car and drove away.

"Dinnertime," Dad said.

We shifted out of human shape, spread our wings, and flew, bat-like, following him to his home. When he stepped out of the car, at the end of the driveway in front of his mansion, we swooped down, shifted form again, and pounced.

The look of terror in his eyes was a wonderful appetizer.

"Not too much," Mom said as we each drank our share. "We don't want to turn him into one of us."

"Yeah," Dad said. "Imagine what a greedy vampire he'd be."

"But I'm glad he's a greedy human," I said as I wiped a dribble of blood from my chin.

"For sure," Rebecca said. "You can really taste the extra cranberry sauce." That was her favorite, too.

"And the pumpkin pie," Cam said. "Turkey Day blood is my favorite blood of the year."

"Even better than Halloween," I said. I licked my lips and enjoyed the lingering flavors of the holiday.

We shifted again and flew off, leaving the man passed out in his driveway. He'd live. But he'd have a monster of a headache when he woke and the memory of some really terrifying dreams. And maybe next year, he wouldn't steal food from those who really needed it.

But I wasn't worried. I knew someone else would show up to take his place at the center of our next family Thanksgiving celebration. If there's one thing you can count on, it's human nature.

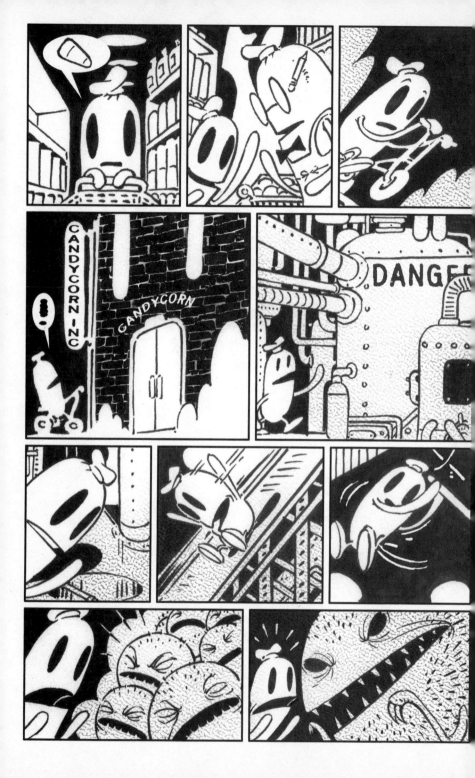

CANDY CORN

My eyes grew wide.

My jaw dropped.

A tiny gasp shot from my throat.

I stared at the words on the sign and clenched my fists.

Temporarily out of stock.

The sign was taped to the bottom of an empty shelf that should have held bags of the best treat in the world.

"It's no big deal, Valerie," Mom said. "We'll get something else for the candy dish. Oh, these look nice." She reached for a bag of chocolate kisses.

"No," I said. "There's nothing else like them."

Mom tossed a bag of kisses in the shopping cart and moved down the aisle. I stared at the empty place as if I could make the missing candy corn appear. It didn't, of course.

I had to do something. I loved candy corn. I loved the way it tasted, the way it smelled, and the way it looked. I even loved the *clickety-tink* sound it made when you grabbed a handful from the glass candy dish. While Mom was sifting through two dozen identical bags of salad greens, in search of the best one, I walked over to the customer service desk, in search of answers.

"Can I help you?" the man on the other side asked.

"There's no candy corn," I said. "It's almost Thanksgiving, and we have to buy candy corn."

The man gave me a sad smile.

"I know how you feel. I love it myself. But the manufacturer is out of it. They had some sort of production problem at the factory. We have to wait for a new supply."

"How long will that take?" I asked.

"It's hard to guess," the man said. "It could be next week. Or even next month?"

"Next month?" I said in a louder voice than I'd planned. "That will be Christmastime."

The man shrugged. "Sorry. There's nothing I can do about it."

Well, if he couldn't do anything, I decided it was up to me to fix things. When we got home from the market, I looked up the candy corn company, Sweet Tooth Confections. It was just outside of town. That was close enough for me to get there on my own. Right after breakfast the next morning, I hopped on my bike and headed out.

The factory was a small brick building down a side road. There were a couple of cars in the parking lot, so I figured it was open. I pedaled up to the door, hopped off my bike, and turned the knob. It opened.

"Hello?" I called. Nobody answered. I walked inside. There was a small room with a desk. Nobody was there, either. At the back of the room, I saw a door with PRODUCTION LINE written on it.

I went through it and found myself at one end of a short hallway. I walked along it. "Hello?"

Still no answer.

The hallway led to another small room with a hole in the middle of the floor. I walked up to the hole and bent over it. I saw what looked like a sliding board.

"Weird," I said. But there was no other way to get anywhere. I had to use the slide, or give up and go home. I'm not a quitter. I stepped on the slide, then dropped to a sitting position.

"Whoa!" I shouted. I hadn't planned to shout, but it was a slick slide. It was a lot more slippery than any slide I'd ever been on.

It was also a long, steep slide. By the time I reached the end, I was zooming so fast the wind was buzzing in my ears. There was a ramp at the end like on a ski jump. I got launched into the air, right toward a rope with a handle on the end. It looked like some sort of zip line. I  grabbed the handle and zipped across the room. I wasn't sure whether to laugh or scream, so I let out a whoop that could have been either of those things.

That's when I saw them.

And when they saw me.

They looked like large rocks, lined up all along the room, filling shelves on either side of me. That was really weird. It got weirder when the rocks opened their eyes.

They had huge eyes, the size of basket-balls.

They had much huger mouths. They all

opened their mouths. Thousands of white pointy teeth glistened at me. The monsters howled and leaped at me.

I hung on to the handle.

There was a terrifying, deafening crash right behind me. I looked over my shoulder. The monsters on either side all crashed into each other, each pair just missing me as I passed them. They bounced back, right to the spot where they'd leaped from. Their eyes spun like they were dizzy.

Something shot in the air and then showered down on me. I heard thousands of *clinkey-clicks* as they fell to the floor.

"Yay, it works again!" someone shouted as my wild ride came to an end at a ledge and I let go of the handle.

A door opened, and people ran into the room, carrying hoses. I guess the hoses were part of a vacuum system. The people sucked up all the monster teeth. I snatched one before it could be pulled away.

"Candy corn?" I asked, staring at it. It looked like candy corn. The white tips were  what I'd seen in the monsters' mouths. I sniffed it. It smelled like candy corn. I took a tiny nibble.

It was delicious!

"Thank you!" one of the workers yelled from below. "They'd been unproductive for weeks. We couldn't get them to leap. Our old line-zipper retired, and nobody else seemed to have what it takes. Your scream is the perfect pitch."

"You're welcome," I said. Even as I watched, new teeth were growing in the monsters' mouths. "Doesn't it hurt them to lose their teeth?" I asked.

"Nope. They enjoy it," the man said. "Right?"

The monsters all nodded and grinned.

"Want a job?" the man asked.

"What do I have to do?" I asked.

"The same thing you just did," the man said.

I thought about the frightening ride. I didn't have to think for long. "Sure," I said. "That would be fun." And I was deliciously good at it.

ABOUT THE AUTHOR

DAVID LUBAR credits his passion for short stories to his limited attention span and bad typing skills, though he has been known to sit still and peck at the keyboard long enough to write a novel or chapter book now and then, including *Hidden Talents* (an ALA Best Book for Young Adults) and *My Rotten Life,* which is currently under development for a cartoon series. He lives in Nazareth, Pennsylvania, with his amazing wife, and not too far from his amazing daughter. In his spare time, he takes naps on the couch.

ABOUT THE
ILLUSTRATOR

BILL MAYER is absolutely amazing. Bill's crazy creatures, characters, and comic creations have been sought after for magazine covers, countless articles, and even stamps for the U.S. Postal Service. He has won almost every illustration award known to man and even some known to fish. Bill and his wife live in Decatur, Georgia. They have a son and three grandsons.

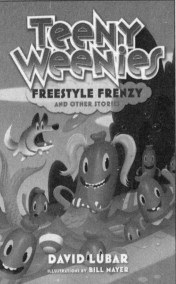